Saturdays and Teacakes

Published by
PEACHTREE PUBLISHERS, LTD.
1700 Chattahoochee Avenue, Atlanta, Georgia 30318-2112
www.peachtree-online.com

Art direction by Loraine M. Joyner

Manufactured in China

10 9 (hardcover)

10 9 8 7 6 5 4 3 2 1 (hardcover and CD package)

10 9 8 7 6 5 4 3 2 1 (CD)

Paintings created in watercolor on 100% rag acid-free paper. Text typeset in Baskerville Infant
and titles in Goudy Gumdrops Old Style.

Library of Congress Cataloging-in-Publication Data
Laminack, Lester L., 1956-
  Saturday and teacakes / written by Lester Laminack ; illustrated by Chris Soentpiet.-- 1st ed.
    p. cm.
Summary: A young boy remembers the Saturdays when he was nine or ten and he would ride
his bicycle to his Ma'am-maw's house,
where they spent the day together mowing the lawn, picking vegetables, eating lunch, and mak-
ing delicious, sweet teacakes.
ISBN 13: 978-1-56145-303-0 / ISBN 10: 1-56145-303-X book
ISBN 13: 978-1-56145-513-3 / ISBN 10: 1-56145-513-X book and CD package
ISBN 13: 978-1-56145-514-0 / ISBN 10: 1-56145-514-8 CD
  [1. Grandmothers--Fiction.] I. Soentpiet, Chris K., ill. II. Title.
  PZ7.L1815 Sat 2004
  [E]--dc22
                                              2003019139

In memory of Zella Mozelle Thompson, my Mammaw
(who would know that every word of this is true),
and for Momma,
Mary Jo Laminack

—*L. L. L.*

With love to Margaret Quinlin and Lester Laminack
for their dedication and passion.
Thanks to my models Luke Fuller and Mary Jo Laminack for bringing the
characters to life, and much appreciation to the town of Heflin, Alabama.

—*C. S.*

Saturdays and Teacakes

Story by
Lester Laminack

Paintings by
Chris Soentpiet

Ω
PEACHTREE
ATLANTA

When I was nine or ten years old I couldn't wait for Saturdays.

Every Saturday, I got up early, dressed, and rolled my bicycle out of the garage.

Every Saturday I coasted down our long steep drive, slowing only enough to make the turn onto Thompson Street, then left onto Bells Mill Road.

Pedal, pedal, pedal, past Mrs. Cofield's house.

Pedal, pedal, pedal, around the horse pasture and up the hill past the cemetery where my grandfather was buried.

Pedal, pedal, pedal, past Mrs. Grace Owens's house and on up to Chandler's Phillips 66.

Every Saturday I coasted over the black hose by the gas pumps just to make the bell ring. Then I dropped my kickstand and checked the air in my tires.

I stopped at Chandler's for another reason too. That's where I crossed the highway that ran right through the center of our town.

My mother always said, *You stop and you look both ways when you get to Chandler's. I don't care if the light is green. I'll hear about it if you don't.*

And I knew she would too. In our little town everyone knew everybody...and told everything to anyone who would listen. So I always looked both ways.

Pedal, pedal, pedal, across Ross Street. Then left for a slow coast down behind the Bank of Heflin, where I turned right onto Bedwell and *whoosh!* I zoomed downhill as fast as I dared.

Pedal…pedal…p-e-d-a-a-a-l-l-l—up the next hill and left onto Almon Street. It was a long stretch to Mr. White's. I always stopped there to catch my breath in the shade of the old oak tree.

One more small hill, pedal, pedal, pedal, and then a right onto Gaither Street. Now I could see my grandmother's drive.

One...

two...

three...

four driveways and one last turn to the left. This was where my tires gave up their humming on pavement and began the crunching of gravel. Just before reaching Mammaw's back porch, I slammed on my brakes, sending a shower of tiny pebbles into her flowers.

Every Saturday Mammaw was there, sitting on her old metal glider—*criiick-craaack-criiick-craaack*—sipping a cup of Red Diamond Coffee and waiting. She was waiting for me. No one else. Just me.

Every Saturday Mammaw called out, *Come on into this house. Let's have us a bite to eat.*

In Mammaw's big kitchen, sunlight poured through the windows like a waterfall and spilled over the countertops, pooling up on the checkerboard floor.

Every Saturday she had hot biscuits, sweet butter, and Golden Eagle Syrup waiting on the kitchen table. Every Saturday she poured a little coffee in my cup and filled the rest with milk and two spoonfuls of sugar.

Then before long Mammaw said, *We best clear these dishes away and get at that yard before it gets too hot.*

I followed her out to the back porch. *Let me put a little water on these ferns,* she said. *You go on ahead to the car house.* (That's what Mammaw called the garage.) *I'll be out directly.*

By the time I pulled the old lawn mower from the garage, Mammaw was already in the garden picking plump, ripe tomatoes for our lunch.

Every Saturday I pulled the starter rope again and again while the mower sputtered and spit. Finally, that old mower started and I struggled to push it through the dew-wet grass, leaving row after row of fresh stripes on the lawn.

From time to time the mower choked on mouthfuls of wet grass that clung to the blades and to my bare legs. But by early afternoon the dew-pearls were gone, the grass was mowed and dry, and I was soaked with sweat.

Every Saturday I pushed the mower back into the garage, trudged to the back porch, and flopped onto that old glider— *criiick-craaack-criiick-craaack.*

Mammaw soon appeared with a tall glass of sweet iced tea. *You just cool off and rest a spell. I'm gonna make us a bite to eat.*

Before long she came back with two big tomato sandwiches on hamburger buns. Every Saturday I gobbled mine down like a hungry dog, but she nibbled at hers like a bird.

Now them's some good tomatoes, she said. *I know how you like a good tomato sandwich. Don't they taste a whole heap better when you've just picked 'em?*

We sat there a while listening to the calls of blue jays and the rhythm of that old glider.

Then Mammaw looked at me sort of sideways and said, *I reckon I know a boy who'd like something sweet to eat.*

And I grinned.

Yes ma'am, I reckon you do.

Come on then, Mammaw said, heading toward the door. *Let's get in this kitchen and see if we can't make us a mess.*

Every Saturday she spread a cloth over the red countertop and scattered a fistful of flour across it, sending a cloud into the air. Then she set out a big bowl.

Mammaw dipped a china teacup into the canister of flour, scooped out a cupful, and skimmed over the top with her finger. Then she dumped the flour into the bowl and added sugar from her black cookie jar. She let the mixture drift through her hands like I sifted sand at the beach.

When it felt right Mammaw said, *Look in the Frigidaire* (that's what she called her refrigerator) *and find me two sticks of Blue Bonnet.*

I pulled open the refrigerator and got out the margarine. I unwrapped the sticks and dropped them into the bowl. I mixed and mashed and mixed and mashed until the ingredients disappeared into a paste. It was smooth and pale yellow and smelled like fresh cotton candy at the county fair.

Mammaw pinched off a little to taste. *I 'spect we need a bit more sugar in this.* She sprinkled sugar until the dough tasted just the way she thought it ought to. *Now get me three eggs,* she said.

I tapped the first egg too hard, making it splatter onto the counter and down the outside of the bowl.

I reckon we can call that half an egg, Mammaw said. *Here, let me show you how to do it. Just tap 'em easy-like and pull the shell apart over the bowl…like this. Now you do the next one.*

It was hard work blending those eggs into the mix with a long wooden spoon.

Mammaw pinched another taste. *My goodness, buddy, we didn't put no vanilla in here. Reach up in that cabinet and get me down the bottle of vanilla flavor.*

When the dough tasted just right, Mammaw rolled it out on the flour-dusted cloth. Then I cut out the teacakes with the rim of an old tin can.

We carefully lifted the circles onto a cookie sheet and put them in the oven to bake—375 degrees for fifteen minutes.

Those fifteen minutes seemed
to last forever.

Are they ready, Mammaw?
Not yet, buddy.

Are they ready now, Mammaw?
Not yet, buddy. Let's give 'em
a little bit longer.

Are they ready yet, Mammaw?
I reckon they might be.

She opened the oven door,
and the kitchen filled with a smell
sweeter than summer gardenias—
the smell of teacakes.

Every Saturday I reached for
one still steaming on the baking
sheet.

You better wait, buddy. They gonna
be mighty hot just yet.

We waited until the teacakes were cool enough to lift from the baking sheet. Then we set them off on a plate.

Every Saturday I ate one, and then another, and I looked at Mammaw.

Is that all you want, buddy? You be sure to eat all you want. We made them teacakes just for you.

When I had eaten all I could, she set a few off on a saucer for herself and put the rest on a big sheet of aluminum foil. She folded the edges into a little handle at the top.

Now you put these out there in your bicycle basket so you won't forget 'em.

Every Saturday as I pedaled over the gravel again and out Mammaw's drive, I glanced back over my shoulder.

Every Saturday Mammaw was there, sitting on her old metal glider and waving. She was waving to me. No one else. Just me.

Don't worry, Mammaw. I won't ever forget.

*F*or Mammaw Thompson's
delicious teacakes recipe,
please visit us at
peachtree-online.com/ teacakes.htm